This Walker Book belongs to:

____

____

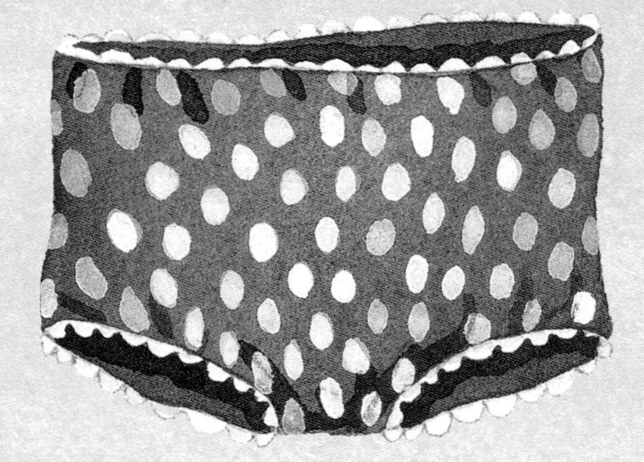

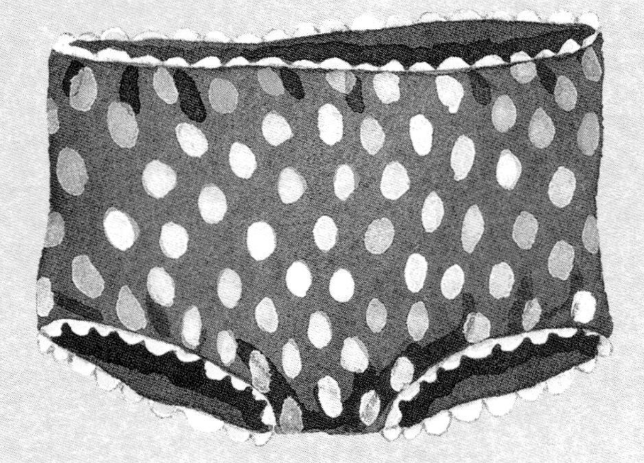
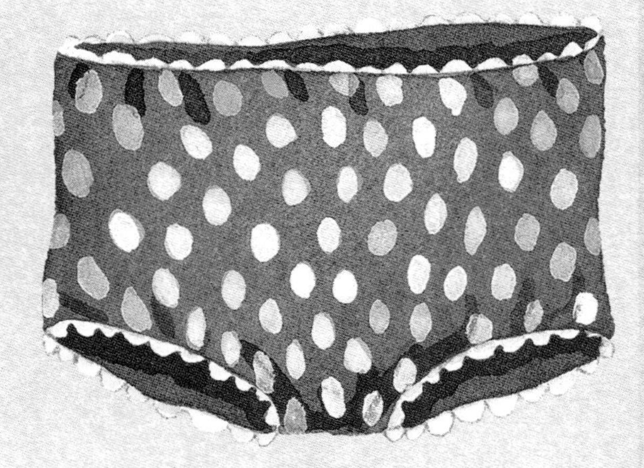

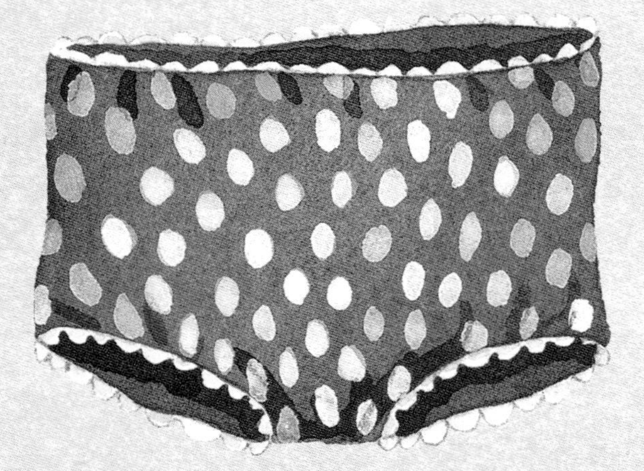
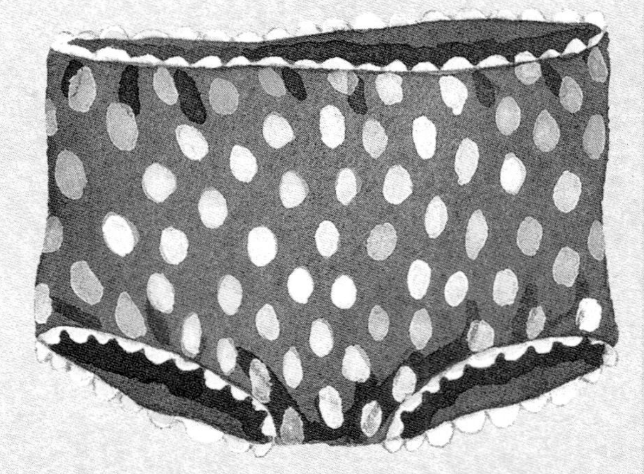

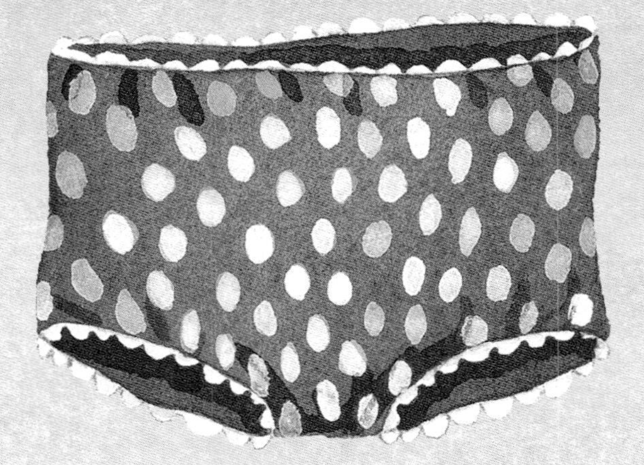
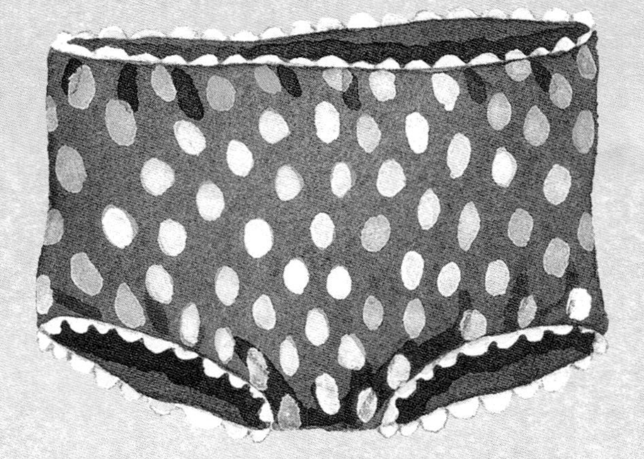
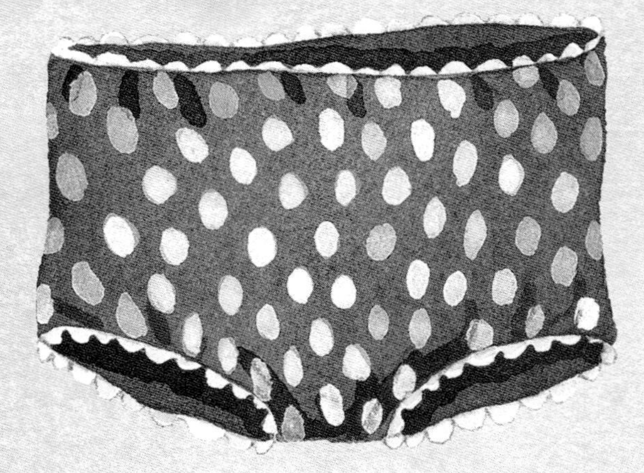

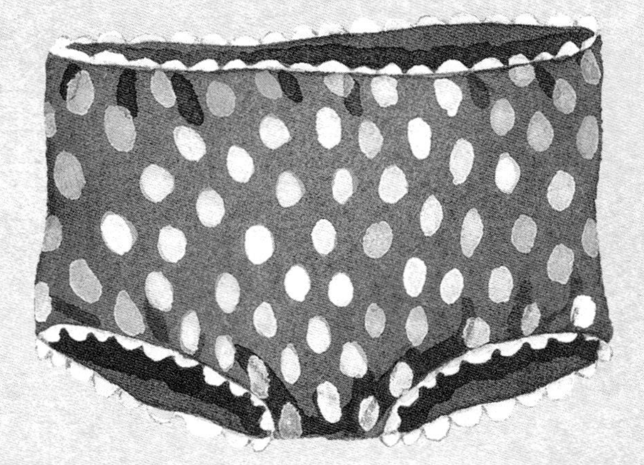

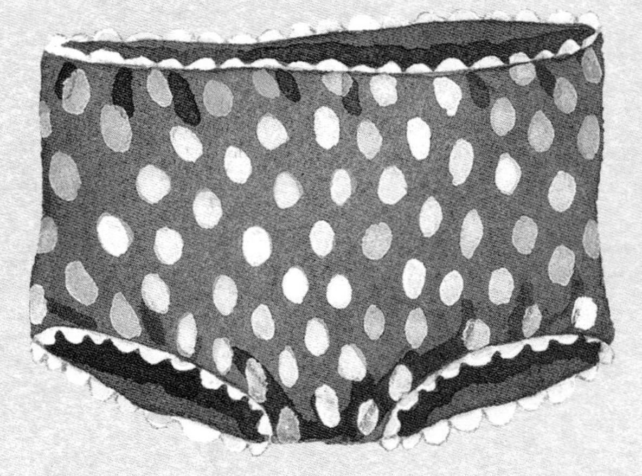

For Rachel – J.E.

To the twins – V.C.

First published 2010 by Walker Books Ltd
87 Vauxhall Walk, London SE11 5HJ

This edition published 2011

2 4 6 8 10 9 7 5 3 1

You can find out more about Jonathan Emmett's books
by visiting his website at www.scribblestreet.co.uk

This book has been typeset in Contemporary Brush

Printed in China

British Library Cataloguing in Publication Data: a catalogue record
for this book is available from the British Library.

ISBN 978-1-4063-2959-9

www.walker.co.uk

THE PIG'S KNICKERS

Jonathan Emmett

Vanessa Cabban

WALKER BOOKS
AND SUBSIDIARIES
LONDON • BOSTON • SYDNEY • AUCKLAND

It was a beautiful spring day on Hilltop Farm and all of the animals were out enjoying the sunshine. All of the animals except Pig, who was feeling sorry for himself.

Look at me, Pig thought, gazing glumly at his reflection, *I'm so drab and dull. If only I looked a little more special.*

As Pig stood there, a gust of wind blew across the hilltop and pulled a pair of polka-dot knickers from the farmer's washing line. The wind carried the knickers across the farmyard and dropped them onto Pig's head.

Pig grunted and was about to toss
the knickers away, when he had an idea.
They're rather special, he thought,
and not at all drab or dull.
I think I should try them on!

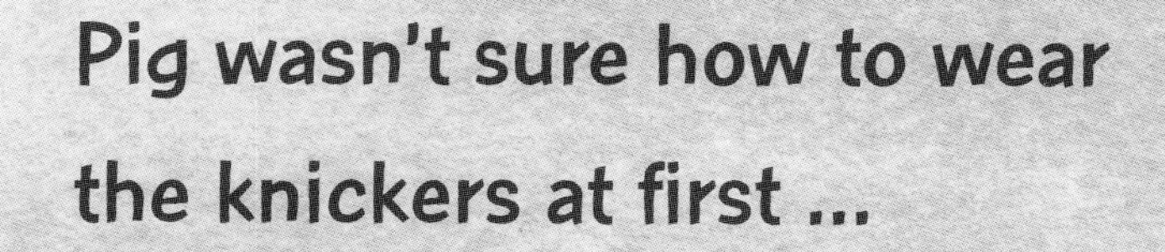

Pig wasn't sure how to wear the knickers at first ...

and even after he'd worked it out ...

he still had trouble getting into them ...

but once they were on, he was tremendously pleased with them!

"They're just my size," he declared, "and the perfect colour for me!"

Pig was so thrilled with his new knickers that he decided to show them off.

Sheep was in the meadow when Pig paraded past.

"Morning, Sheep!" said Pig, marching around the meadow.

He snatched up a stick and twirled it in front of him,
tossing it high into the air.
"What do you think of me in my new knickers?"
he asked as he strutted past.

Sheep was lost for words.
"Amazing!" she said at last.

Pig was so pleased that he decided to show off to Cow as well.

Cow was in the barn when Pig pirouetted past.

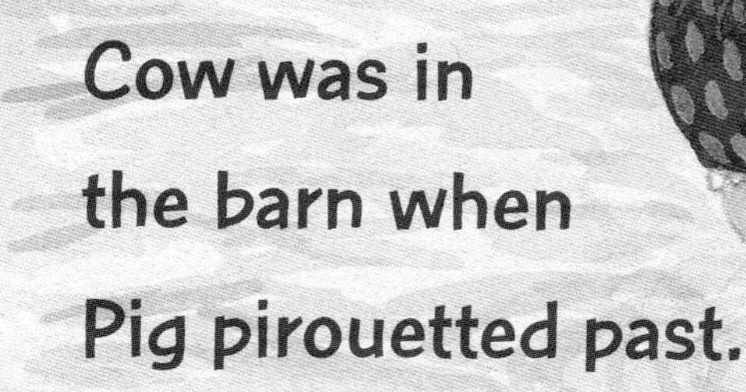

"Hello, Cow!" said Pig, break-dancing across the barn floor.

Then he tangoed around the tractor and danced the salsa through the straw. "What do you think of me in my new knickers?" he sang as he shimmied away.

Cow was flabbergasted. "Astonishing!" she said at last.

There was no stopping Pig now.
He wanted the whole world
to see how wonderful he looked
in his new knickers.

Goat was in the farmyard when
Pig pranced past.
"WOTCHA, GOAT!" cried Pig,
cartwheeling around the cowshed.

He back-flipped up onto the washing line and tightroped to the other end. "WHAT DO YOU THINK OF ME IN MY NEW KNICKERS?" he shouted as he somersaulted back to the ground. Goat was so stunned, he stopped eating for a moment.

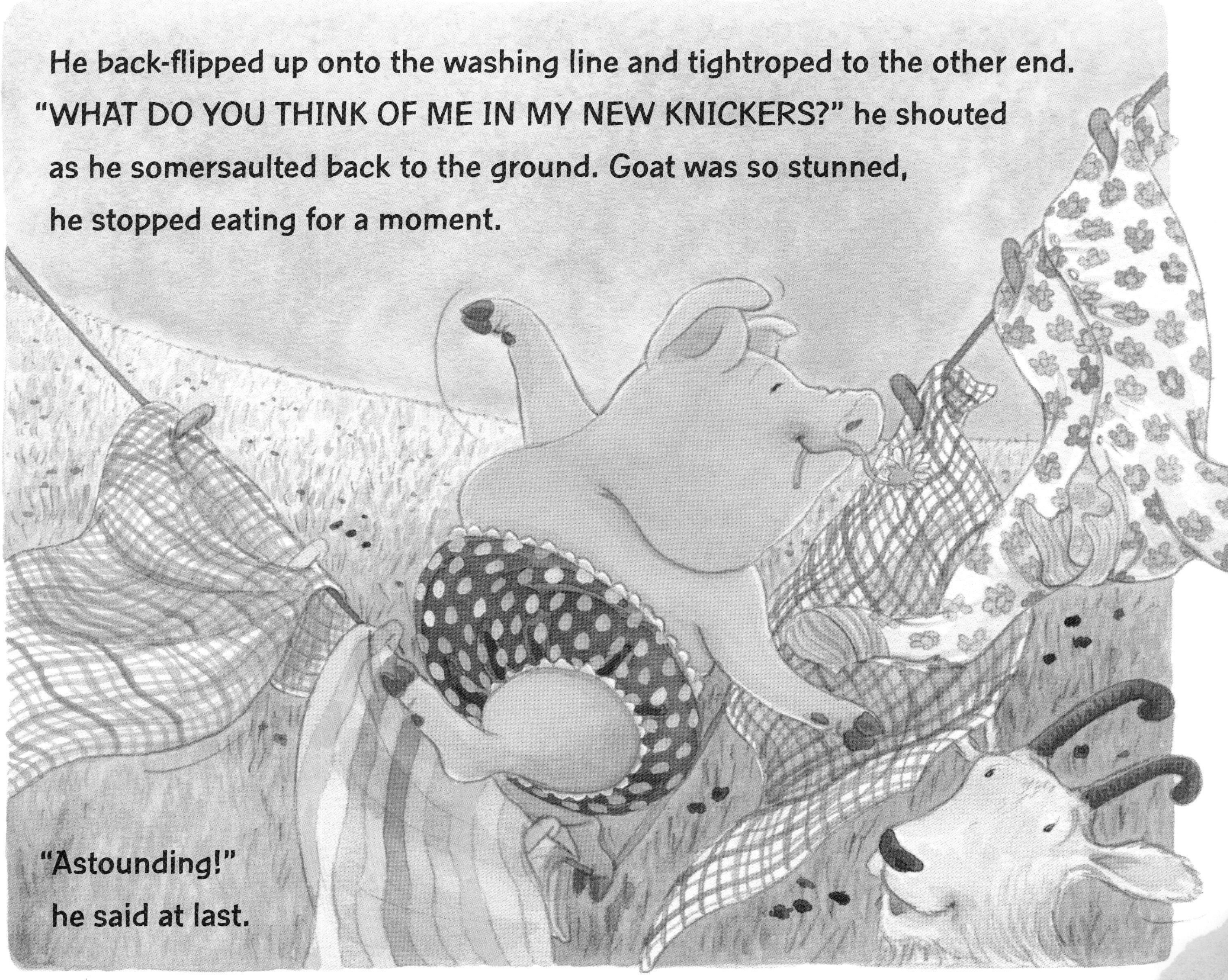

"Astounding!" he said at last.

Pig was so proud of his knickers
that he wore them everywhere.
But they were so dirty by the end of the day
that he had to take them off
to give them a wash.

Pig hung the knickers up to dry
and settled down to sleep.
He slept soundly that night,
dreaming of his wonderful
new knickers.

But Goat was too hungry to sleep,
so he got up to find
something to eat.

Goat found something
hanging on the side
of Pig's pen.

It was too dark to see
what it was ...

but it didn't taste too bad.
So Goat gobbled it down.

The next morning the farm was woken by a terrible cry.
"MY KNICKERS! MY KNICKERS!
I'VE LOST MY KNICKERS!"
wailed Pig.
All the other animals ran to Pig's pen
and found Pig in floods of tears.
"I hung them up to dry
and now they're gone," he sobbed.
Everyone tried to cheer Pig up,
but he was inconsolable.

"But they were my SPECIAL knickers,"
said Pig. "Without them,
I'm just drab and dull. With them,
I was AMAZING
and ASTONISHING
and ASTOUNDING!
You said so yourselves!"

"But Pig," said Sheep, "it wasn't your knickers
that were amazing, it was YOU!"
"Yes," agreed Cow, "it was what you were
doing in them that was astonishing."
"You would have been just as astounding
without them," added Goat,
who looked rather guilty
about something.
"Do you really think so?"
said Pig, a grin spreading across his face.

"Do you really think that I'm special – even without my knickers?"

"ABSOLUTELY!" said all the other animals.

Once Pig had found that he was still special, he was very happy.
And, later that day, Pig found something else that made him happier still.

"I don't need knickers to be special," he told the other animals.

"And especially now
that I've got a new..."

"BRA!"

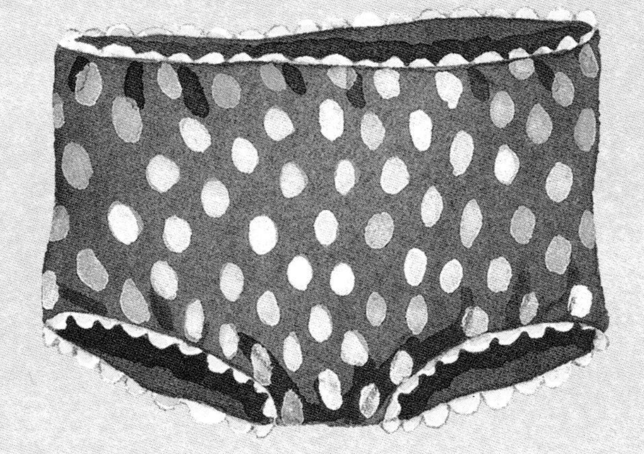
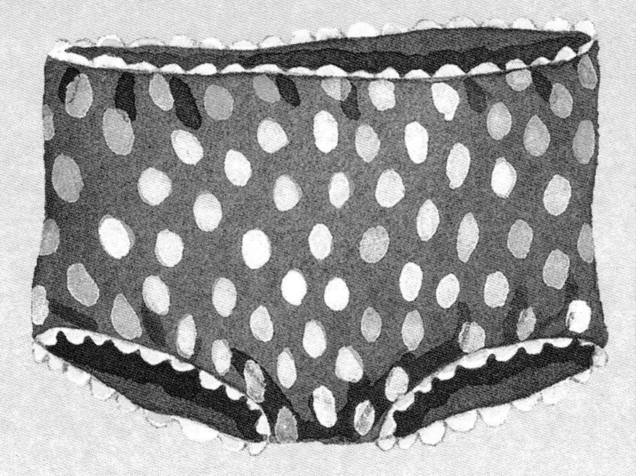

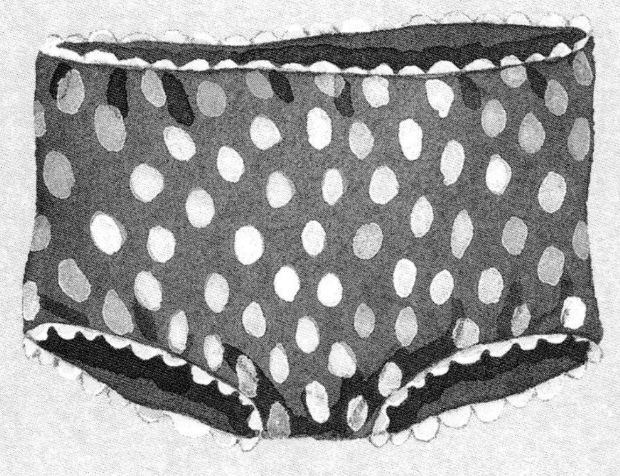

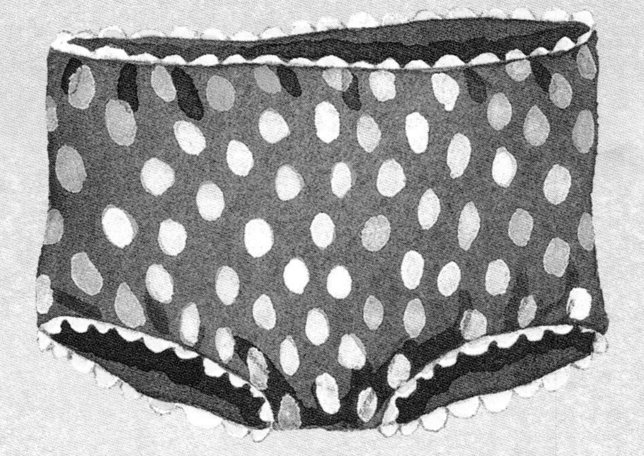
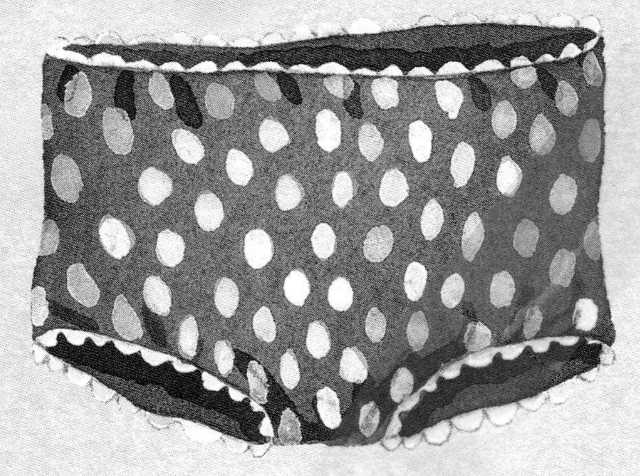

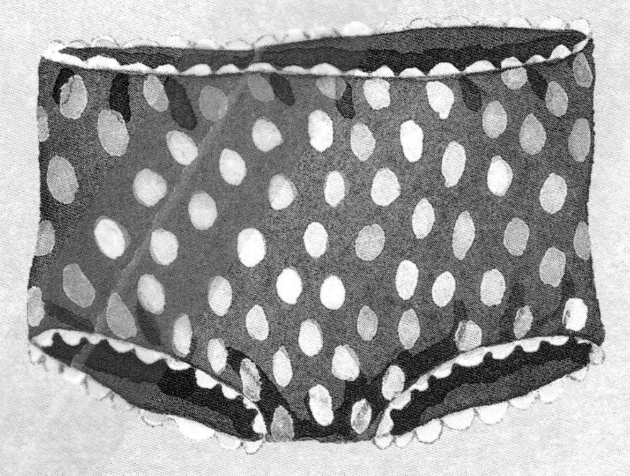

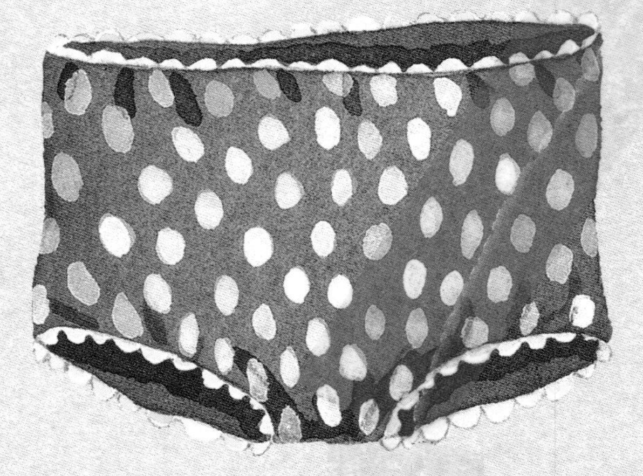

Also by Jonathan Emmett and Vanessa Cabban

Meet the Mole who thinks a lot...

ISBN 978-0-7445-8950-4
ISBN 978-1-84428-521-1
ISBN 978-1-4063-1957-6
ISBN 978-1-4063-0596-8